The Mystery of the Eagle Feather

THE THREE COUSINS
DETECTIVE CLUB

———————

The Mystery of the Eagle Feather

Elspeth Campbell Murphy

Illustrated by Joe Nordstrom

BETHANY HOUSE PUBLISHERS
MINNEAPOLIS, MINNESOTA 55438

Cover and story illustrations by Joe Nordstrom

Three Cousins Detective Club is a trademark
of Elspeth Campbell Murphy.

Published by Bethany House Publishers
A Ministry of Bethany Fellowship, Inc.
11300 Hampshire Avenue South
Minneapolis, Minnesota 55438

Printed in the United States of America.

Library of Congress Cataloging-in-Publication Data

CIP applied for

ISBN 1–55661–412–8   CIP

In loving memory of my father-in-law,
Howard R. Murphy,
whose life was filled with
love, joy, peace,
patience, kindness, goodness,
faithfulness, gentleness, and self-control.

ELSPETH CAMPBELL MURPHY has been a familiar name in Christian publishing for over fifteen years, with more than seventy-five books to her credit and sales reaching five million worldwide. She is the author of the best-selling series *David and I Talk to God* and *The Kids From Apple Street Church*, as well as the 1990 Gold Medallion winner *Do You See Me, God?* A graduate of Trinity College and Moody Bible Institute, Elspeth and her husband, Mike, make their home in Chicago, where she writes full time.

Contents

1
Indian Stuff

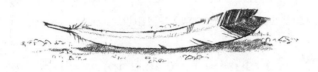

"**W**ow, Tim!" said Timothy Dawson's cousin Titus McKay. "Your room looks like a giant lives in it. All your stuff is up so high!"

"It's Priscilla," said Timothy. "Trust me. If she can reach it, she'll wreck it. And she's just learning how to open doors."

"She is *so cute* the way she does things!" exclaimed Timothy's other cousin, Sarah-Jane Cooper. (Neither she nor Titus had a baby sister.)

Timothy didn't comment, except to make a growling noise in the back of his throat.

He didn't go around saying so, but he actually thought Priscilla was a sweet kid.

The problem was, Priscilla thought Timothy was *wonderful.* And therefore, she thought all of his stuff was wonderful, too. She was forever trying to get her sticky little toddler fingers on anything that belonged to her big brother.

For some reason, she particularly liked his Indian stuff. Timothy had some neat Indian stuff.

Some of it had come from a good friend of his—an Indian boy he had never met. Never in person, that is. But he and Anthony Two Trees had been writing letters to each other for almost a year now.

It had all started as a project for school. Timothy's class had been studying American Indians. And Timothy had discovered that, next to art, social studies was his favorite subject.

His teacher had arranged to have the class write letters to a class of Native American kids.

The other kids had each written one nice letter and gotten one nice letter back. And that was that.

But Timothy and Anthony had discovered they had a lot in common. For one thing, they both liked baseball. For another thing, they both liked art.

And when you put those two things together, you get decorated baseball caps. Timothy's was usually covered with metal slogan buttons—though sometimes he wore it "plain." Anthony's was beaded.

So they had kept on writing letters to each other.

Timothy told Anthony about his cousins and how they had a detective club and solved mysteries.

Anthony told Timothy about learning Indian dances and competing at powwows.

Then, for his final social studies project, Timothy had made a model tepee from scratch, with only a little help from his parents.

Timothy had been tempted to paint pictures all over it. But he stopped himself. For one thing, he knew most tepees nowadays were left almost plain. For another thing, the shape of a tepee was so crisp and clean, it didn't need a lot of decoration.

So Timothy had controlled himself and just added a couple of touches. He painted a band of eagle feathers around the top. He painted a band of turtles around the bottom. And then—in honor of his friend—he painted two trees by the door flap.

Timothy's model tepee was a work of art, if he did say so himself.

Timothy's teacher said the tepee was exquisite and gave it an A+.

Timothy sent Anthony a picture his father had taken of Timothy, Titus, and Sarah-Jane around the A+ tepee.

The picture had turned out to be funny, though. That was because you could see Priscilla off to one side reaching out to grab the tepee. And you could see Timothy's mother's arm reaching out to grab Priscilla.

Timothy wrote to Anthony that he knew Indians didn't live in tepees anymore. He enclosed a gift of special beads an artist friend had given him.

Anthony wrote back to say that Indians did sometimes still live in tepees. For the weekend, anyway, when they went to powwows.

Anthony said Timothy's model tepee was just right. He especially liked the two trees by the door flap.

And Anthony enclosed a picture of himself in his powwow outfit. He had put Timothy's

beads in a position of honor in the center of his headband.

Anthony had designed the outfit himself. His mother had sewn it, and Anthony had added most of the decorations.

Enclosed with the letter were some genuine elk teeth and porcupine quills.

"I wish you could come see me dance in person," wrote Anthony.

"I wish I could, too," Timothy wrote back.

And that's how he got his Great Idea.

2

An Educational Vacation

"*A* powwow!" Timothy's parents had said when Timothy suggested it. "What a Great Idea! Very Educational."

Educational. It was a word the cousins had been hearing a lot lately.

Earlier that year the parents had all gotten together to plan their vacations.

Now that Timothy, Titus, and Sarah-Jane were ten, the parents had decided the cousins were old enough to go on vacation with one another.

And now that the cousins were ten, the parents had decided that these trips should be Educational—with a capital E.

"A powwow!" the aunts and uncles had said. "What a Great Idea!"

That's why Titus and Sarah-Jane were at Timothy's house now. They were going out west with Timothy's family. And as part of the trip, they were going to visit a powwow to meet Anthony Two Trees.

Titus and Sarah-Jane wanted to see the model tepee up close again. So Timothy got out the step stool and got the tepee down. He wished he could take it to show Anthony in person. But there was no way to pack it so that it wouldn't get wrecked.

Timothy showed his cousins the elk teeth and porcupine quills that Anthony had sent him. He showed them the picture of Anthony in his dance-contest outfit.

"So cool!" said Sarah-Jane. "I wish I had an outfit just like that."

"Sorry, old pal," said Timothy, patting her shoulder. "Only men and boys can be grass dancers. But there are some neat-O contests for women and girls, too. I got a book out of the library that tells about powwows. You won't believe the costumes!"

He got the book off the shelf, and the cousins poured over the pictures, ooing and ahing at the designs and colors.

"Actually," said Timothy, correcting himself, "you're not supposed to call them costumes. The dancers aren't dressing up like anyone else. They're just wearing what they're supposed to wear for the kind of dance they do.

"There are some rules about what the different kinds of outfits are supposed to look like. But after that, the dancers can decorate their outfits any way they want to. In fact, the judges give points for the decoration, not just the dancing.

"It took Anthony hours and hours and hours to decorate his. But even so, he's just a kid with a kid's outfit. He says the really professional dancers have outfits that are worth hundreds—even thousands—of dollars."

"Hmmm," said Titus, as if he was thinking it over. "I don't think I have *quite* that much spending money. But didn't you say there will be booths where we can buy some great Indian stuff? I know *exactly* what I want to buy."

"What?" asked Timothy and Sarah-Jane together.

"An eagle feather," declared Titus. "Just like the ones Anthony is wearing on his head."

"Sorry, old pal," said Timothy, patting him

on the shoulder. "There's no way you can buy an eagle feather."

"Why?" asked Titus. "Too expensive?"

"No," said Timothy. "It's against the law."

"What?" asked Titus. "You mean because eagles are an endangered species?"

"Bingo," Timothy replied. "The only people who can own eagle feathers are Indians. And even they can't *buy* them. They get them free from the government. When an eagle dies in the wild or in the zoo, the feathers are stored away. Indians can write and ask for eagle feathers to use on ceremonial outfits. But they can't sell the feather or give them away to non-Indians like us."

"So—" said Titus. "Those really fancy outfits with eagle feathers all over them—even if you had a bazillion dollars, you couldn't buy one?"

"Not legally," said Timothy.

"Well, what do you know?" said Titus with a heavy sigh. "I'm crushed. But at least I can say I learned something new today."

Sarah-Jane groaned. "This trip is so Educational, we're learning stuff before we even get out of the house!"

It sounded like grumbling from his cousins, but Timothy knew it wasn't.

Titus and Sarah-Jane loved the powwow idea as much as his parents and aunts and uncles did.

It made you feel pretty important to have everyone love your Great Idea.

But it could also make you feel a little nervous, Timothy realized. Because—what if it didn't work out? What if something went wrong?

Relax! Timothy told himself. *Going to a powwow is a Great Idea. What can possibly go wrong?*

3

At the Powwow

*W*hen they got to the town where they would be staying, Timothy's father rented a car so that they could drive to the powwow the next day.

They got up early and drove for miles and miles.

Titus, who lived in the city, kept looking around as if wondering where they kept the buildings out here. "Now I know what they mean by wide, open spaces!" he said.

It was beautiful country. Timothy had never seen anything like it except in pictures.

And when they got to the powwow, it was as if the pictures in Timothy's library book had come to life.

Timothy almost thought he was going to

faint. Not from the heat—though it *was* hot. But from the excitement.

They saw trailers and campers and tents of all kinds. But rising above them all were the tepees. Bright white cones with crisscrossed poles pointing toward the sky. Some of the poles still had pine branches on the top that waved in the breeze. And some of the tepees were decorated with gorgeous designs.

At the center of it all was a huge, round open area—the arbor—where the dancing would take place.

Dancers, with big contest entry numbers pinned to their outfits, streamed toward the arbor in a river of colors. It was almost time for the Grand Entry.

Timothy caught his breath. It was almost more than the artist in him could stand. He wanted to run around, flapping his arms and yelling—as if that could maybe help him take it all in.

But he controlled himself and scanned the crowds of dancers for Anthony. There wasn't time to find Anthony's camp before the Grand Entry. So the family went to find seats.

Suddenly, Timothy was jostled by someone coming the other way.

That someone was a dancer, and the sight of him made Timothy gulp. He was dressed in the traditional style with buckskin fringes and a big eagle feather bustle at the back of his waist. His feather headdress was so big you could hardly see his face. And the part of his face you could see was heavily painted.

"Excuse me," said Timothy, though it was

more the dancer's fault than his.

The man didn't answer but hurried away and disappeared from sight among the tepees.

"Nice guy," said Sarah-Jane. "Why is he going that way if the dance arbor is this way?"

"Must have forgotten something, I guess," said Timothy. "Come to think of it, it *did* seem like something was missing from his outfit."

His cousins stared at him in disbelief.

"The guy was covered from head to foot in feathers and beads!" exclaimed Titus. "You couldn't even see his face. What could possibly be *missing* from an outfit like that?"

"I don't know," murmured Timothy. "But I'm sure something was."

4

A Snatch of Conversation

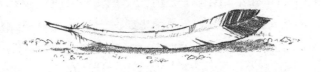

Sometimes really unbelievable things happen. Like when you go to a powwow far, far from home and sit down right in front of people who used to live next door to you.

"Paul?! Sarah?!" said a couple of amazed voices behind Timothy's parents.

"Bill?! Judy?!" cried Timothy's parents, turning around. "What are *you* doing here?"

"What are *you* doing here?"

There was still a little bit of time before the Grand Entry. And the grown-ups had already started to fill it with talk about remodeling their kitchens. So Timothy asked if he and Titus and Sarah-Jane could go buy souvenirs.

His parents said OK, as long as they stayed together and kept an eye on the time.

It was a point of honor with the cousins that they could be trusted to do stuff on their own without getting into trouble. They had figured out pretty early on that they didn't need people to make them behave if they could make themselves behave. And their parents knew they could count on the cousins to behave. So it all worked out really well.

It was a good thing they didn't have a whole lot of time at the booths. Otherwise, Timothy never would have been able to make up his mind what to buy. As it was, he went with his first impression and bought a beaded V-shaped harness to wear over his shirt. Titus trusted Timothy's judgment and bought the same thing, except with a little bit different design. Sarah-Jane bought some brightly colored beaded necklaces that she piled on top of one another.

They still had some money, so they bought feathers to wear on their heads. Not eagle feathers. No amount of money could buy those. So they had to be content with dyed chicken feathers. Actually, the final effect was pretty impressive—if they did say so themselves.

Even after buying the feathers, the cousins still had some money left. So they put it together and spent it all on Priscilla. They bought her a little rag doll wearing a jingle dress outfit. There were little metal cones sewn in rows around the dress. When you shook the doll to make it "dance," the cones clinked together in a jingle sound. Priscilla would love it.

The cousins were just paying for the doll when they noticed a small group of worried-looking people huddled together nearby. The cousins overheard snatches of their conversation.

And what they heard made them prick up their detective ears:

"A terrible thing!"

"Are you sure he didn't just misplace it?"

"He says no, that he knows exactly where he left it."

"And now it's gone?"

"Gone!"

"He blames himself, poor man, for leaving it unattended."

"But who would take something like that?

He shouldn't blame himself."

"And no one saw a thing?"

"Not a thing."

"But with so much going on—"

"How can you replace something like that?"

"You can't. It's priceless.."

"It was in his family for generations."

"That's right."

"And now he says he'll never dance again."

"A terrible thing!"

"Who would do something like that?"

Suddenly the conversation was cut short by the sound of drums. The Grand Entry was about to begin.

"What was that all about?" asked Titus as they rushed back to their seats.

"It sounds like something was stolen," said Sarah-Jane. "But what?"

"Beats me," said Timothy with a worried frown.

It was the second mysterious thing that had happened that day. And the powwow hadn't even officially started yet.

5

The Grand Entry

*W*ith the pounding of the drum it was hard to think of anything else. The singers sat in a circle around the big drum and pounded out the rhythm. Then they began to sing.

It was time for the Grand Entry.

First came the honor guard, carrying the flags. Then came people who served in the military. Then came the young women who had been crowned powwow princesses.

Timothy felt Sarah-Jane squirm beside him. From the look on her face, he could tell she was dying to be an Indian princess.

The adult dancers came next, stomping and twirling to the rhythm of the song. The honor guard moved to the center of the arbor so that as more dancers came in, they formed a big, spiral circle.

"EXcellent!" gasped Titus.

"So cool!" breathed Sarah-Jane.

"Neat-O!" agreed Timothy. The Grand Entry was one of the most exciting things he had ever seen. It was all the more exciting because coming to the powwow had been his Great Idea, and it was all working out so perfectly. Well, almost perfectly.

Timothy looked for the dancer who had so rudely run into him. But he couldn't pick him out. There had been something odd about him, Timothy was sure of that. He just didn't know what it was.

The kid dancers came after the adults. Timothy could see them lined up by the entryway, waiting their turn in line to dance into the arbor.

He got out his photograph of Anthony and studied it carefully. Then he strained to see if he could spot Anthony in person amid all those colorful outfits.

He might not have seen him if Anthony hadn't been scanning the crowds in the stands to get a glimpse of Timothy at the same time.

Timothy and Anthony spotted each other at exactly the same moment. They smiled and waved. Timothy nudged Sarah-Jane and Titus, who smiled and waved, too.

Then Anthony turned his attention to dancing. He looked as if he was concentrating very hard. Timothy even thought he looked a little worried. But he couldn't imagine why.

When Anthony danced into the arbor, the long yarn of his outfit waved as smoothly as grass on the prairie waving in the wind. His movements were so controlled and so free all at the same time. Maybe Anthony could show him how to do it.

At the end of the line came the tiniest dancers, some of them not much older than Priscilla.

"Oh, Aunt Sarah!" cried Sarah-Jane. "Couldn't you just *die*? They're *so cute*! Look, Priscilla, look! Little girls just like you. And they're wearing jingle dresses just like your dolly!"

After the opening ceremonies, everyone was invited to dance.

Timothy caught sight of Anthony making his way through the crowds toward him. He

hoped Anthony would show him how to do at least a couple of steps.

But Anthony's first words were a complete surprise. "Timothy! Thank goodness you're here. Can you come back to the camp with me right away? I need the T.C.D.C."

6

The T.C.D.C.

"*W*hat's a 'teesy-deesy'?" asked the old man who met the children at the camp.

"It's letters, Grandfather," said Anthony respectfully. "Capital T. Capital C. Capital D. Capital C. It stands for the Three Cousins Detective Club. This is my pen pal, Timothy Dawson. I told you all about him."

"Ah, yes," said his grandfather. "The boy who made the tepee and who sent you beads for your dance outfit. How do you do, Timothy?" he asked, politely shaking hands.

"And these are his cousins Sarah-Jane Cooper and Titus McKay."

The old man shook hands with Sarah-Jane and Titus as well.

Anthony said, "Mother has invited Timothy's parents and baby sister to eat supper with us after the contests. But I asked Timothy, Titus, and Sarah-Jane to come back to the trailer with me before I have to dance. They're very good at finding things. I thought they could help me look for John's eagle fan. I saw him wandering around all by himself. He looked very upset."

He turned to the cousins. "Eagle feathers are very special to us. We are not supposed to let them touch the ground. If an eagle feather should fall from someone's outfit during the dancing, the dancers form a circle around it to protect it. An elder is called to come pick it up. That's why John is so upset about his lost fan."

He added, "John is my uncle. But he's only a few years older than I am. He hasn't been dancing all that long. But now he's so upset, he wants to quit."

"Yes," said Timothy. "We overheard some people talking about it. They said how terrible it is that it was stolen."

"Stolen!" cried Anthony and his grandfather together. "What makes you think it was stolen?"

"Well, wasn't it?" asked Titus, sounding confused.

"Not that we know of," said Mr. Two Trees. "We just assumed my son had misplaced it. He is still a teenager, and sometimes young people can be careless. Although—I have never known him to be careless with his dance outfit before. . . ."

Sarah-Jane said, "The person we heard about was *sure* something of his had been stolen. We didn't hear what it was. Just that it was priceless and had been in his family for generations."

Mr. Two Trees just shook his head sadly as if he couldn't think of the words to say how he felt about that.

"Those people couldn't have been talking about John," said Anthony. "He made the fan himself. It was new. Besides, he was so embarrassed about losing it that I don't think he would have told anyone."

Timothy said, "I'm beginning to think your Uncle John didn't misplace his fan at all. Two valuable things missing in one day? It's just too much of a coincidence."

7

Just Looking Around

"**I**f there is a thief at work, then we must alert the powwow police," said Anthony's grandfather. "I'll go find John, and we'll do that now."

The cousins and Anthony watched him go.

Timothy sighed. "Well, I guess it's out of our hands."

"Not necessarily," said Anthony. "We can still have a look around. I mean, I'm sure the police will do what they can. But if there's a thief, he'll be watching for any sign of the police and get scared off. But we're just kids. We can go where we want to, and no one will think twice about it. We can pretend I'm showing you around, and I will be. But *really* we'll be looking for anything suspicious."

The cousins looked at one another and smiled. Here was someone who thought the way they did.

Anthony said, "We need to get a good view. Can you ride?"

"Ride?" asked Timothy. "You mean like a bicycle?"

"No, silly," laughed Anthony. "A horse. All the kids around here can ride. I know someone who will lend us some horses."

"I can ride," said Sarah-Jane, who lived in the country and whose neighbor had a horse.

"Do you need a saddle?" asked Anthony.

"No," said Sarah-Jane. "Either way."

"Good," said Anthony. "All the kids around here just ride bareback."

In the end they decided that two horses were enough. Timothy had once ridden a pony at a carnival, but that didn't really count. So he climbed up behind Anthony and held on tight. Titus had never ridden a horse at all. But the horse seemed to really like him, so that worked out OK. Titus climbed up behind Sarah-Jane.

They didn't try anything fancy. Just let the horses walk casually through the campground.

It was fun. But it was also disappointing. They didn't see anything at all suspicious. Still, something was tugging at the back of Timothy's mind.

When they returned the horses, Anthony said, "Well, it was worth a try. I don't want you to miss any more of the dancing. Besides, my group is up soon, and I'd better get going. Is my number on straight?" He pointed to the big entry number hanging on his outfit and laughed. "When you've practiced as hard as I have, you at least want the judges to see your number."

"You look great," said Titus.

"Perfect," said Sarah-Jane.

"Perfect," echoed Timothy.

It wasn't until Anthony had gone and they were wandering back to the stand that a sudden thought hit Timothy.

An outfit could be perfect and still have something missing.

8

No Number

"*T*here was no entry number!" Timothy said to his cousins.

"What?" asked Sarah-Jane, sounding confused at this announcement out of the blue.

"What are you talking about, Tim?" asked Titus.

Timothy tried to control his excitement long enough to explain what he meant.

"Remember that dancer who ran into me? And how I said there was something missing from his outfit? Well, I just figured out what it was. There was no big entry number attached to his outfit."

"But that doesn't make sense," said Sarah-Jane. "The judges need to see those numbers to keep track of the dancers."

"Right," said Titus. "And don't the dancers need to pay an entry fee when they get their numbers? I don't think a dancer would even be allowed to compete without one. Are you *positive* that guy didn't have a number? I mean, why would someone get all dressed up like that if he wasn't going to be in a dance contest?"

"Yes," said Sarah-Jane. "Those outfits must be awfully hot. Why would you be covered from head to foot—even painting your face—on a day like today if you didn't have a really good reason?"

Suddenly Titus and Sarah-Jane came to a full stop and stared at Timothy, openmouthed.

Timothy said, "My point exactly."

9

A Brilliant Theory

"*L*et me make sure I have this straight," said Sarah-Jane. "You think the guy who bumped into you isn't a dancer at all? That he's—what? Just some guy *disguised* as a dancer?"

"I looked for him in the Grand Entry, and I didn't see him," said Timothy. "I know that doesn't prove anything, but no dancer wants to miss the Grand Entry. So—let's just say he *is* just some guy in disguise. He could walk around the campground and no one would think anything of it. He could pick up John's fan and carry it around, and it would just look like part of his outfit."

"I think you're on to something, Tim," said Titus. "I wonder if the headdress was the other thing he stole? It *did* look a little too big for him, didn't it?"

Timothy nodded. "The headdress. The fan. Who knows what else? The point is, if you're wearing shorts and a T-shirt and an eagle feather headdress, people are going to look at you funny. But if you're all dressed up as a dancer, everyone will assume everything you're wearing, everything you're carrying is yours."

"And," added Sarah-Jane, "if your face is all painted, how could anyone tell who you are? For all we know, this guy might not even be an Indian."

"He probably isn't," said Timothy. "I don't think an Indian would steal a powwow outfit. If he tried to wear it as his own, he would run the risk of it being recognized. Besides, would an Indian treat eagle feathers that way?"

Titus said, "So our best guess is that the thief is someone who couldn't get eagle feathers legally, is that it? Someone who might sell them to people who didn't care where they came from. Some people always want what they can't have. I mean, come on, folks. Let's show a little self-control."

They were all quiet for a few moments, thinking about all this.

Then Titus said, "But what do we do now? Go up to the police and say, 'Officer, arrest that man—he's not wearing a number!'? I don't think so."

"And he was also so rude!" exclaimed Sarah-Jane indignantly.

The boys laughed, and she had to admit that sounded funny. You couldn't arrest someone for being rude.

Then all three of them realized they had to admit something else:

They had a brilliant theory . . .

And not a shred of proof.

10

Refreshments

"*T*here you are," said Timothy's mother as they climbed back into the stands during a lull in the program. "Did you have a good time with Anthony? You missed the Inter-Tribal dance. You should have seen Priscilla. We took her down to the edge of the arbor, and she was dancing with the other toddlers. She really got into the excitement of things."

Sarah-Jane opened her arms wide and Priscilla crawled onto her lap. "Did you dance, little sweetie-face?" Sarah-Jane asked her. "Oh, you're just the cutest little baby in the whole wide world, aren't you?"

"S-J, please!" groaned Timothy.

"Well, she is!" said Sarah-Jane staunchly. "Aren't you, Priscilla?"

Priscilla nodded happily.

The cousins sat in a row, not saying much. It was a funny feeling to have so much on your mind and yet not feel ready to talk about it.

The grown-ups were no longer talking about remodeling kitchens. They had moved on to talk about remodeling bathrooms.

Timothy wondered if a person could actually die of boredom.

Then he realized that he wasn't bored. He was restless. And he was restless because he was itching to do something about the thefts. But what?

Then the drumming started up again, and it was hard to think of anything else.

This was Anthony's contest, and Timothy felt a surge of pride. It was almost like being down there with him. He felt a lot less restless when the dance was over.

Anthony ended up with third prize, which wasn't bad at all. There had been a lot of good competition.

Timothy found himself wondering about Anthony's Uncle John. He hoped he wouldn't give up dancing because of his missing fan.

Anthony must have been able to put his

worries about his uncle out of his mind, Timothy thought. It sure seemed Anthony was concentrating on his dancing. Or maybe it was that he was dancing *for* his uncle. Timothy remembered Anthony once telling him that a dancer sometimes dedicated a dance to someone who needed help. Anthony had said that you always dance better when you're dancing for someone else.

Timothy wished he had a way to help.

His father's voice broke into his thoughts. "How about a snack? What does that sign down there mean—Indian fry bread? What's that? And what are Indian tacos? Let's go find out."

The food helped. It almost always lifted Timothy out of his crankiness.

But what helped his crankiness even more was to look up and see "that guy" calmly eating at the next picnic table.

11

Out for a Stroll

*T*imothy casually drummed his fingers on the table. It was a secret signal he had with his cousins for when it wasn't safe to talk. It meant: High alert! Look around carefully. But don't say anything!

Very, very casually, Titus and Sarah-Jane looked around. Then Titus adjusted his glasses, and Sarah-Jane scratched her nose. That meant: Message received. We see what you see.

The guy was wearing a different headdress and a simpler outfit, but the face paint was the same.

There was no sign of John's fan.

What was he doing? Stashing the stuff somewhere and coming back for more?

"I see a little girl who needs a nap," said Timothy's mother as Priscilla rubbed her eyes. "Maybe I should put her in her stroller and walk her around. Maybe she'll drop off to sleep."

"We'll do it," Timothy volunteered.

He gave a long, slow stretch, which meant: Follow my lead.

"Sure," said Titus. "I feel like walking around some more, anyway."

"Sounds like fun," said Sarah-Jane.

"Oh, would you?" said Timothy's mother, obviously pleased. "That will give me some more time to visit with Bill and Judy."

The topic was now Water in the Basement. Who could resist *that*?

Fortunately, Priscilla was not in one of her me-do-it moods, where she insisted on pushing the stroller herself.

That would have ruined The Plan.

As it was, she got into her stroller without a fuss.

And when the guy at the next table got up to leave, he never suspected a thing.

He didn't even notice that he was being followed at a safe distance.

Followed by three nice kids, who just happened to be out for a stroll with a baby.

12

Tepees

*B*efore long they were joined by a fourth nice kid. Anthony, now dressed in jeans and a T-shirt, caught up with them.

Timothy said, "Hey, you were great out there!"

"Yeah?" said Anthony with a happy grin. "Thanks! What are you guys doing now? Just taking your baby sister for a walk?"

"I'm glad it looks like that," replied Timothy. "Because we're also 'keeping a suspect under surveillance.' " (It was a phrase he had heard on T.V., and he had always wanted to use it.)

"Who's the suspect?" asked Anthony.

So the cousins filled him in on their theory.

"Wow!" said Anthony. "Do you really

49

think he's the thief? Grandfather said the police had gotten quite a few complaints about things being missing. And if that guy is the thief, where do you suppose he put all the stuff? He doesn't have it with him."

"You're right about that," said Timothy. "I'm beginning to think this is a wild goose chase."

No sooner had he said that than a truck went rumbling along the dirt road, stirring up a lot of dust. They closed their eyes, coughing and spluttering. When they looked again, the suspect had disappeared among the cars and tepees.

"As I was saying," sighed Timothy. "A wild goose chase. I don't know—should we tell the police we saw a suspicious-looking character? When you come right down to it, the only thing suspicious about him was that he wasn't wearing a dance number."

Anthony shrugged. "It wouldn't hurt, I guess. I don't know if they have much else to go on. If you like, I'll go talk to them now and catch up with you later."

"Sounds good," said Timothy. "We'll walk Priscilla around a little more. I want to see those tepees up close, anyway."

"Tepee! Tepee!" said a little voice from the stroller.

"Well, look who's not taking a nap like she's supposed to. Come on, Sib. Let's go look at some real tepees. And then you have to go to sleep."

Sib was Timothy's pet name for his sister. It was short for *sibling,* a word that meant a person's brother or sister. Timothy thought Sib also sounded like it could be short for Priscilla.

"TEPEES!"

"OK. OK."

"You know—" said Titus slowly as they walked among the tepees. "If a person wanted to hide a bunch of Indian stuff, a tepee would be a pretty good place to do it."

Sarah-Jane agreed. "Because the stuff would just look like it belonged there."

Timothy said, "And both times we saw the guy, he was headed toward the tepees. So maybe he *is* using a tepee for a hiding place. The problem is—which one?"

13

A Clue on the Ground

*T*here was one tepee standing apart from the rest and a little ways off the road. The cousins strolled over to look at it.

There didn't seem to be anyone at home, and the cousins were dying to peek inside. But they knew better than to go barging into places.

They were just turning to leave when Priscilla got all excited about something on the ground. She bounced up and down. She stretched out her hands the way she did when she was trying to grab Timothy's stuff.

"Birdie! Birdie!" she cried.

"*Birdie*?" said Timothy. "What are you talking about, Sib?"

He took a closer look. There on the ground

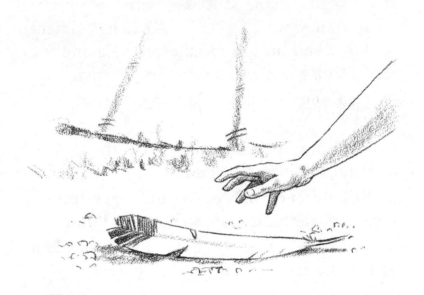

near the tepee door lay a magnificent eagle
feather.

Timothy almost reached down to pick it
up, but he pulled back just in time. He remembered that they were guests at this powwow.
And picking up an eagle feather was a job for
an elder of the tribe.

So the cousins—with Priscilla in her
stroller—stood in a circle around the eagle
feather to protect it.

They looked around for someone to help.
Most everyone was at the arbor, watching the
dancing.

But they were in luck. At that moment Anthony and his grandfather came along the road. With them was a young policeman.

"Anthony!" called Timothy. "Over here. Quick!"

Anthony, his grandfather, and the policeman hurried over to them.

Still no one came out of the tepee. Either someone was hiding, or no one was home.

Old Mr. Two Trees gave a little gasp when he saw the eagle feather on the ground.

But he smiled at the cousins standing in a circle around it. "You did well, my children," he said. "You did well."

Anthony said, "How do you suppose the feather got here? Do you think it could have fallen off of something that was stolen?"

"It's certainly possible," said Titus.

"We thought the guy we saw might have hidden the things around here."

The young policeman stepped to the door of the tepee.

"Hello," he called. "Hello. Is anyone home?"

Getting no answer, he lifted the door flap and looked inside.

"Well, I'll be!" he exclaimed. "Grandfather Two Trees, please come look at this."

14

The Give-Back

"*H*i!" said Timothy's mother. "You kids were gone awhile. Did Priscilla take a nice nap?"

"No," said Timothy. "She didn't sleep a wink. She was too busy tracking down clues and recovering stolen treasure."

It took a while—quite a while—to explain what he meant by that.

The tepee had indeed been a storage place for stolen items, people's most treasured things.

But the thief was nowhere to be found.

Titus had a theory that maybe he had dropped something off and gone away. Then when he came back, he saw a policeman at his door and knew he had to get out of there. *Fast.*

He probably had a car somewhere nearby.

Everyone said the theory made sense. But they would never know for sure.

The cousins had been able to give the police a very good description of the man's outfit. They were able to describe the face paint. But all the guy had to do was wash his face and change into street clothes. And then—who would know? He would just look like anyone else.

But at least they had found the hidden treasures.

And now the problem was tracking down the rightful owners.

That's when Anthony had suggested a give-away.

"A *what?*" the cousins had all said at once.

"It's a custom we Indians have," said Anthony. "It's for when we want to celebrate something important that has happened to us. Or for when we want to honor someone in our family. We collect gifts all year to bring to a powwow. Then we spread them out in the arbor. Whoever needs them can come and get them. The family is honored by what they give away. And everyone comes up to shake hands and give congratulations. So instead of people giving *us* presents on special occasions, we give *them* presents."

"EXcellent idea," said Titus.

"We think so," said Anthony, smiling. "Anyway, this would not be a giveaway exactly. More like a give-*back*. The police can spread the things out in the arbor. And those people the things were stolen from can come get them back."

"EXcellent idea!" said Titus again.

And everyone agreed that it was.

15

A High Honor

*A*nthony's "give-back" was quickly arranged.

The MC announced to the crowd what had happened and invited the people to reclaim what had been taken. It was a time of overwhelming joy.

Anthony and his grandfather and the policeman and the cousins—including Priscilla, of course!—had to stand in the arbor, because people wanted to shake their hands.

Priscilla got enough attention to last her until she was ready to go to school. (At least, that was Timothy's opinion.)

But the greatest honor was yet to come.

The old man, whose headdress had been stolen and found, heard that Timothy and

Anthony both liked art. So he came up with an idea to mark this occasion. He invited the boys to paint a design on his tepee.

Anthony and Timothy talked it over and decided what they would paint. Two eagles facing each other in lasting friendship.

Then Timothy's family went to Anthony's family camper for supper.

They had a wonderful time. Except that Anthony's parents started telling Timothy's parents about building an addition onto their house. And maybe remodeling the kitchen . . .

"Anthony, old pal," said Timothy. "Why don't you show us some dance steps?"

So Anthony showed the cousins how to do some steps from his dance.

The cousins were really lousy at it. At least compared to Anthony.

It took so much control to keep from falling.

But then it was time to say goodbye. Which was *really hard.*

Anthony and the cousins had only known each other in person for a few hours. But it seemed as if they had known one another forever.

As he walked to the car for the long ride
back, Timothy turned to wave. At the same
moment, he and Anthony called out the same
thing to each other: "Don't forget to write!"

By the time the car was on the open road,
Priscilla was sound asleep.

"There's my sweetie," Sarah-Jane murmured, stroking her little hand. "Did you have
a busy day?"

They had all had a busy day when it came to that.

Timothy could feel himself starting to doze. Titus was already drifting off.

His father said, "This was a Great Idea of yours, son—coming to a powwow."

"Yes, it was," said Timothy. "If I do say so myself. It was very . . . Educational."

The End